To Farmington's fine teachers—
especially Judy Baccei
—JL

To my parents, Geraldine and Martin,
both teachers at schools,
but also my teachers in life
—GR

 little bee books

251 Park Avenue South, New York, NY 10010
Text copyright © 2020 by Janet Lawler
Illustrations copyright © 2020 by Geraldine Rodriguez
Library of Congress Cataloging-in-Publication Data
Names: Lawler, Janet, author. | Rodriguez, Geraldine, illustrator.
Title: Kindergarten hat / Janet Lawler, Geraldine Rodriguez.
Description: First edition. | New York: Little Bee Books, [2020] |
Audience: Ages 3-6. | Audience: Grades K-1. | Summary: Carlos Abredo
loves building forts, playing soccer, and gardening but he does not want
to start kindergarten, until his new teacher reaches out to make him and
his fellow students feel welcome. | Identifiers: LCCN 2019041966
Subjects: CYAC: First day of school—Fiction. | Kindergarten—Fiction.
Classification: LCC PZ7.L4187 Kin 2020 | DDC [E]—dc23
LC record available at https://lccn.loc.gov/2019041966
Manufactured in the United States of America WRZ 0620
First Edition 10 9 8 7 6 5 4 3 2
ISBN 978-1-4998-0989-3
For more information about special discounts on bulk purchases,
please contact Little Bee Books at sales@littlebeebooks.com.

littlebeebooks.com

KINDERGARTEN HAT

by Janet Lawler

illustrated by
Geraldine Rodriguez

"I don't want to go to kindergarten,"
Carlos said as he worked in his garden.
"I won't know anyone there."

On the sign: Carlos's Garden

"New friendships blossom in new places,"
said his mother.

"What if the bus gets lost?" Carlos asked.
"It won't," said his mother.

"What if I can't find my teacher?" he asked.
"You will," his mother replied.

Carlos wasn't so sure.

The next day, the mail arrived while Carlos was practicing his moves. "A letter for me!" he cried.

His mother read it to him:

Dear Carlos,

I hope you are having a fun summer. I will be your teacher this year. On the first day, I will wear a huge, flowered hat.

Please bring a flower for it and a big kindergarten smile. I can't wait to meet you!

Your teacher,
Mrs. Bashay

P.S. Sometime soon, please send me a photo of you doing something you love.

Carlos spent two days deciding what photo
to take and send.

He liked building forts, playing soccer, and vrooming cars.

He liked drawing pictures and fiddling on Mom's phone.

But most of all, he loved gardening—the fun of his fingers in dirt, the surprise of seeds sprouting, and the brightness of the blooms. So, Carlos posed in front of his flowers.

The night before school began, Carlos lay awake
for a long time. When he finally fell asleep,
he dreamed he was lost in a scary forest.

The next morning, Carlos woke early, his tummy twisting and turning. But after breakfast, he rushed out and picked the most beautiful daisy for Mrs. Bashay.

Carlos clutched his flower with both hands. Would Mrs. Bashay like it?
His mother gave him a hug and walked him onto the bus.

Carlos slid into an empty seat and gently set the daisy down. Chatter and laughter filled the air. Everyone seemed to know one another. A lot of the kids were so much bigger than him.

When the bus swayed around a corner, he glanced back and saw a boy holding a rose. The boy smiled and nodded. Then Carlos heard a voice. "He loves me, he loves me not. He loves me, he loves me not!"

An older girl was plucking petals off a daisy.

Carlos looked down. His flower was gone!

"That's mine!" he exclaimed, grabbing it back.

"I'm sorry," said the girl. "I found it on the floor."

"It's ruined!" Carlos squeezed his eyes tight. A tear fell. He tried poking the petals back in place, but they wouldn't stay.

The bus pulled up at school.
"I'm really sorry," the girl said again. "Have a good first day."
Carlos slumped.

The boy with the rose paused in the aisle. "Come on,"
he encouraged, waving Carlos out.
Carlos peered out the window.

Then he saw it—the most magnificent, stupendous, tremendous hat, bouncing and dipping.

The brim tipped up, and he glimpsed a smiling lady.
Mrs. Bashay! Children gathered around her.
They offered her real flowers and ones made of
silk, paper, and plastic. One kid even gave her
a balloon blossom!

Carlos took a deep breath. Then he stepped
off the bus and stood under a tree.

Mrs. Bashay flipped through photos, calling names.
Her students lined up. "Carlos!" she called.
"Carlos Abredo?"

He gave a tiny wave. As Mrs. Bashay approached,
Carlos dropped what was left of the daisy
behind his back.

"Hi, Carlos," she said. "Welcome to kindergarten!"
He sniffled. "I don't have a flower for you . . . anymore."

"That's okay," Mrs. Bashay said.
Carlos pointed to his photo.
"See that big daisy? That was for you."
"It was?" asked Mrs. Bashay.

Carlos took a deep breath. "Maybe . . . maybe we can pretend?"

"What a good idea!" said Mrs. Bashay. She nestled the picture smack in the middle of her hat. "We're going to have a fun year. Let's go start our first day!"

Then Carlos gave Mrs. Bashay the other thing he was supposed to bring to school—a great big kindergarten smile.